The Kids of the
Polk Street School
15

MONSTER RABBIT RUNS AMUCK!

Patricia Reilly Giff

Illustrated by Blanche Sims

A YEARLING BOOK

Published by
Bantam Doubleday Dell Books for Young Readers
a division of
Bantam Doubleday Dell Publishing Group, Inc.
1540 Broadway
New York, New York 10036

ISBN: 0-440-40424-X

Printed in the United States of America

March 1991

20 19 18 17 16 15

CWO

To Jimmy Giff,
who loves the beach,
and who made the summer of '89
terrific.

MONSTER RABBIT RUNS AMUCK!

Chapter 1

"The Beast is home," Richard Best yelled. He raced down the driveway ahead of his sister Holly.

His mother was planting something in the yard.

She smiled and waved at them.

In the kitchen, Beast slung off his backpack.

He dumped everything out on the floor. His math book. A pencil without a point. A bunch of graham cracker crumbs.

"You're making a big mess," Holly said. She put her hands on her hips. "*You're* a big mess."

1

Richard looked down at his new spring jacket.

It had grease stains all over it.

He shouldn't have crawled under that parked car for his ball.

He shook his backpack again.

A comic book slid out. It was all about Leko the Lizard Man.

Most of the time Leko was just a plain person.

Then he'd hear of a crime.

He'd flap his ears over until they disappeared into his head.

He'd press his nose and say "Hizzam."

His nose would disappear too.

Then lizard lumps would pop out all over him.

Leko was ready for anything.

Holly leaned over. She looked at the comic. "What junk you read."

"Leko's the best," Beast said. "He can

2

turn into any color, any shape. Last time he turned into a telephone pole—''

Holly reached for a bag of marshmallow chicks.

She pulled it open. She dumped out the chicks.

''Too bad you don't turn into a telephone pole too,'' she said.

He made a beast face at her.

Then he grabbed a bunch of chicks.

He headed for the living room.

Holly was right behind him.

''I've got the television,'' she said.

Beast popped a chick into his mouth.

It was the best candy in the world.

He watched Holly twist the TV knob.

''Don't eat all those chicks,'' she said. ''Daddy said half and half.''

Beast swallowed. ''You had about a hundred last night. Besides, I can't even find the bag of jelly beans.''

Holly didn't answer. She stared at the TV set.

It was a commercial. *No more goo with Stick On Glue.*

Beast had heard it a thousand times.

A lady with lots of shiny teeth sang the "No More Goo" song.

She snapped her fingers at the same time.

Beast was trying to snap his fingers too. It didn't seem to work though.

Holly was hopping up and down in front of the TV. She waved her arms around and sang, "No more gaaa-loooooo."

She was trying to look like the lady with the teeth.

Instead, she looked like a toothpick. A toothpick with curly brown hair.

"Turn down that TV, will you," he said.

Holly didn't answer.

He knew she wouldn't.

He smoothed out the cover of "Leko the Lizard Man."

4

It was Matthew's comic book. Matthew's little sister had scribbled all over Leko's picture.

Too bad. Beast could just about see Leko turning into a lizard.

Beast folded his own ears down with his fingers. "Hizzam," he hissed.

Holly turned to look at him. "Why are you doing that with your ears?" she asked. "Is something wrong with you?"

Beast rubbed at his eye. "Itchy," he said.

He lined up the chicks on the floor. Then he lay back.

"I just remembered," Holly said. "I have to talk to Mom."

She narrowed her eyes at him. "Don't touch the TV. I'll be right back."

Beast turned the comic book page.

Leko had turned into a curtain. He was listening to someone talking on the phone.

Beast knew the man on the phone was a criminal. He had a horrible look on his face.

"Mom!" he heard Holly yelling.

The back door slammed. Holly was gone.

Beast chomped one of the chicks in half.

He looked through the rest of the Leko book.

At the end Leko won.

Leko always won.

Beast ate the last chick. Then he went into the kitchen.

He still couldn't find the jelly beans.

Holly had hidden them somewhere.

He went upstairs slowly. He slid along the way Leko would.

He sneaked into Holly's bedroom.

"You can't fool me," he said. "They're under the bed."

He leaned over to look.

No jelly beans.

He could hear Holly. She was coming up the stairs, coming fast.

He opened the closet door. He slid inside.

It was dark in there. Messy too.

He stepped on something.

He could hear it crunch.

He reached down to see what it was.

It was an egg carton. A sparkly pink egg carton.

It was flat now.

Some of the sparkles had stuck to Richard's shoe.

Holly must have made it in Art.

Beast was supposed to bring an egg carton to school this week too.

He pushed Holly's carton under a pile of clothes.

Outside everything was quiet. He wondered why he didn't hear Holly walking around.

He pushed the door open.

Holly wasn't in the bedroom.

She had gone right past.

She was sitting on their parents' bed. The telephone was in her hand.

Beast crept out to hear what she was saying.

7

"Joanne?" Holly wound the cord around her finger. "My mother says it's all right."

He crawled toward the door.

"It'll be the greatest surprise," Holly said. "Don't tell anyone yet."

Beast stood up. What surprise?

Holly started to whisper into the phone.

He leaned forward. He was dying to know what she was saying.

He couldn't hear one thing.

"Don't worry," he said to himself. "Beast the Lizard Man will find out everything."

He laughed a Leko laugh.

He went downstairs to look for the jelly beans.

Chapter 2

The next afternoon, Beast tiptoed ahead of Matthew.

Beast was Leko the Lizard Man. Matthew was his helper, Fleko the Fly.

They started down the basement stairs.

It was so dark they could hardly see.

Matthew slipped on the last step. He started to laugh.

Beast felt like laughing too. He covered his mouth with one hand. He pushed open the laundry room door.

They rushed inside.

Safe!

They could just about see into the play-room.

Holly was waving her arms around.

Behind her Joanne was stuffing her mouth with a chick.

"What nerve," he said under his breath. "Eating all my stuff."

". . . food's going to be all right," Joanne was saying.

Holly nodded. "Food's going to be great."

"See," Beast whispered. He hardly moved his lips. "I told you they had some kind of secret."

". . . your brother," Joanne was saying.

". . . eats like a gorilla," said Holly.

Matthew gave Beast a poke. He started to make gorilla noises. "Unk, unk."

Joanne stood up.

"Shh," Beast said. He tried not to breathe.

Joanne poked her head out the playroom door. "Do you hear something?" she asked Holly.

"Don't be afraid," Holly said. "It's safe in here."

"Thought I heard something." Joanne sounded worried. "It almost sounded like a gorilla."

"It's only the furnace," said Holly. "Don't worry. It used to scare me to death when I was little."

Beast snorted. Holly was the biggest scaredy-cat in the world. She still wouldn't stay alone in the basement for half a second.

Joanne went back. She sat down on the other side of the playroom.

Beast could hardly hear her.

". . . the party," she said. "What are we . . ."

". . . likes games," said Holly. "Especially Parcheesi."

Beast sat back. A party. Holly was having a party.

It wasn't her birthday.

It wasn't Joanne's.

They both had summer birthdays.

Beast fanned his face with one hand.

It was really getting hot in that laundry room.

It smelled of soap powder and old clothes.

He could tell Matthew was getting sick of hanging around in there too.

Matthew was rooting through the clothes in the basket.

He kept throwing them up in the air.

He tried to catch them with one hand before they landed back in the basket.

"Let's get out of here," he said finally. "I can't breathe."

"All right," Beast said.

He stood up and started down the hall ahead of Matthew.

"I'm sure I heard—" Joanne began.

"Don't be—" Holly broke off. "I hear something too." She started to scream. "It's a killer."

Beast and Matthew raced for the stairs.

14

"Come on, Fleko," Beast yelled. "Let's fly out of here."

They banged out the back door and into the yard.

"Watch out for the tulips," Beast shouted. "My mother will—"

He looked down.

He had just landed on a fat pink one.

He took a step back, then stood still.

"Hey, Matthew," he said. "Guess what? My birthday's this month."

Matthew took his foot off a yellow flower. "Happy birthday," he said.

Beast shook his head. "I can't believe it. Holly must be giving me a party."

He stood there for a moment. "Isn't that something? My first surprise party."

Chapter 3

The next day was Art.

Ms. Rooney's class marched down the hall.

Beast and Matthew were last.

"Hey," Matthew said. "I forgot my egg carton."

"Me too," Beast said.

He thought back to supper last night.

Holly was talking about her carton.

"Gorgeous," she said. "I'm going to keep all my jewelry inside."

Beast snorted. Holly's jewelry was junky. As junky as the carton.

He swallowed.

Wait till she took the carton out of the closet.

Wait till she saw what he had done.

Maybe she'd skip his party.

The class rushed into the Art room.

All the windows were opened.

"Smell that good spring air," said Mrs. Kara.

Beast looked at Matthew.

Ms. Rooney was always smelling the good spring air too.

Beast slid into a seat.

"How many forgot their egg cartons?" Mrs. Kara asked.

Beast raised his hand.

So did Matthew.

Mrs. Kara tapped her long red fingernails on her desk.

She was frowning.

Beast knew it wasn't a real frown though.

Mrs. Kara never got angry about anything.

"Look in my closet," she said.

Beast and Matthew raced to the back of the room.

Beast banged into the closet door. "Beat you." He gave Matthew a punch in the back. "Get it? Beat you like an egg."

Mrs. Kara looked up. "Let's not run amuck in the Art room," she said.

"Amuck, amuck," Beast whispered.

Matthew laughed. He opened the closet door.

On the shelf was a pile of egg cartons.

Matthew reached for them.

"Make sure there's no egg glop stuck to mine," Beast said.

"Let's not take forever," said Mrs. Kara.

Matthew grabbed an egg carton.

He tossed one to Beast.

They quick-stepped back to their seats.

"Now," said Mrs. Kara. "This is what we're going to do."

She stopped. "Wait a minute. I think you two shouldn't sit next to each other."

Beast looked at Matthew. He knew Mrs. Kara remembered last week.

He and Matthew had started a pencil race.

Everyone else in the class had been looking at pictures of famous artists.

Beast went over to sit near the window.

There was an empty seat behind Jason Bazyk.

"Pay attention now, please," said Mrs. Kara. She held up an egg carton.

It was painted a bright purple.

Yellow diamonds sparkled on the top.

It was the silliest thing Beast had ever seen.

He looked at the inside of his carton.

"Look at that," he whispered to Jason. "Egg glop all over the place."

"How lovely these will be for our colored eggs," Mrs. Kara said, smiling.

Beast made believe he thought it was lovely too.

At the same time, he flapped his ears over with his fingers.

He pressed his nose.

"Hizzam," he whispered.

"Hizzam?" Sherri Dent asked. She looked as if she thought he was crazy.

Quickly Beast put his hands down.

That Sherri was some pain in the neck.

Just like Holly.

Then he remembered his surprise party.

He wondered if she had sent out the invitations yet.

He gave Jason a little punch. "Are you coming to my party?"

"Sure I will," Jason said. "When is it?"

Beast shook his head. "No, I mean did you get an invitation?"

"No." Jason shook his head slowly. He looked worried.

"Don't worry," said Beast. "You're right on top of the list."

He hoped Holly knew what she was doing.

He hoped she hadn't left Jason out.

Jason was a good friend.

He'd have to make sure she knew that. Somehow, tonight at supper, he'd have to—

Mrs. Kara stopped at Beast's desk.

She put a small bottle of blue paint in the corner. "See," she said. "I remembered your favorite color."

Beast swallowed. "Pink. Do you have any pink left?"

Sherri Dent turned around and looked at him. "Pinky pinky little girl," she said.

Linda Lorca started to laugh.

He hated Sherri Dent.

Linda Lorca wasn't so hot either.

They were going right off his birthday list.

"Pink paint, please," Beast said again.

Mrs. Kara switched bottles.

Beast looked at it. He sighed.

Then he started to splash the color all over the egg carton.

Chapter 4

The bell rang.

It was time to go home.

Beast slid down the stairs.

Matthew slid right behind him.

"I am Leko the Lizard Man," yelled Beast. "I'm running amuck."

"What's going on here?" Mrs. Kettle called from the top step.

Mrs. Kettle was the sixth-grade teacher.

She was the strictest teacher in the whole school.

When she frowned you were in a lot of trouble, Beast thought.

And they were in trouble now.

There was no sliding down the stairs in the Polk Street School.

Mrs. Kettle snapped her fingers.

Beast and Matthew marched up the stairs to her classroom.

The desks were huge in there.

Maps were hanging all over the place.

Egg cartons lined the window sill.

Beast looked at them, surprised.

They were all a mess.

The one he was making for Holly was much better.

He cleared his throat. "My sister is waiting for me—"

He stopped. He didn't want to say he was such a baby he couldn't walk home alone.

Mrs. Kettle stared at him from under her thick eyebrows.

Then she looked up at the clock on the wall.

"You can help me for ten minutes," she said. "Maybe you'll remember to walk next time." She frowned. "Instead of sliding around like a pair of lizards."

Beast looked at Matthew out of the corner of his eye.

He reached up to one ear. He made believe he was going to flap his ears the way Leko did.

Matthew's face turned red.

Beast knew he was ready to laugh.

"Let's see." Mrs. Kettle stared at them. "What could you do?"

She reached for her keys. "Take these—" She looked at Beast. "Stop scratching your ears. That's a terrible habit. Think about washing instead."

Matthew made a little noise in his throat.

"Don't act like a hyena," she told him. "Go down to the auditorium closet. Both of you."

Beast nodded. He didn't dare look at Matthew.

"We have to get that rabbit out," Mrs.

Kettle said. "You know, the big one. He'll stand on the stage for the Spring assembly on Thursday. The first graders are putting on a play."

Beast took the keys.

They raced out of the room.

"Walk!" Mrs. Kettle shouted. "Walk."

They slowed down.

"Don't run amuck," Matthew whispered.

They burst out laughing as soon as they turned the corner.

"Leko is turning into a hyena," said Beast.

"So is Fleko," said Matthew.

They started down the stairs.

Holly was at the bottom.

She looked up at them. "What's the matter with you?" she said. "I've been waiting this whole time—"

"You'll have to wait some more," Beast said. Then he stopped. He smiled at her. "Sorry."

Holly blinked.

"We have to go on an errand for Mrs. Kettle," said Matthew. "An important one."

Holly gritted her teeth. "Hurry up," she said. "I can't wait around all day."

Beast looked at her.

She had the ugliest face he had ever seen.

He wondered if she hated having all those freckles.

He went past her. He followed Matthew into the auditorium.

They marched up the stage steps. Together they crawled under the blue curtain.

"Back here," Beast said.

"I am the world's greatest actor," said Matthew in a booming voice.

"I thought you were Fleko the Fly," said Beast. He turned the key in the lock and swung open the door.

In front of them was the Easter Rabbit.

It came up to Beast's shoulders.

It had cotton stuck all over it, and two huge blue eyes.

27

"What a monster," Matthew said.

"How are we going to get it—" Beast began.

"It's on wheels," said Matthew. "We'll just push him to the front."

Beast looked at the rabbit's carrot. It was full of dust.

"Whew," he said.

"You push," said Matthew. "I'll pull."

The rabbit went faster than they thought. Easier.

It sped across the stage.

Beast slid along in back of it. "The monster rabbit is running amuck," he yelled.

"Watch out, Leko," yelled Matthew. He pulled open the curtain.

"You watch out," Beast began. "Don't let him go off—"

The rabbit rolled faster.

"Catch him," Beast yelled.

Too late.

The rabbit sailed off the stage.

It landed in the front row with a crash.

The head rolled down the aisle.

Matthew and Beast raced after it.

In back of the auditorium the doors opened.

It was Holly.

"That's it," she said. "You two just got yourselves expelled."

Chapter 5

It was the next afternoon.

Beast walked down the street with Matthew.

They were carrying piles of clothes.

Mr. Hunt, Matthew's neighbor, had given them some money.

They were taking his suits to be cleaned.

"You're dragging the pants on the ground," Mr. Hunt yelled from the window.

Beast hoisted up his pile.

He had a terrible feeling inside.

Even the money didn't make him feel better.

"Don't worry," Matthew said. "Mrs. Kettle won't know."

"She'll know," said Beast.

"Don't think Mrs. Kettle knows everything in the whole world," Matthew said.

Beast sighed. He could still see the rabbit's head rolling down the aisle yesterday.

"Listen," Matthew said. "We stuck that head on as good as new."

Beast nodded a little. He knew Matthew didn't believe that.

The head was wobbling all over the place.

Mrs. Kettle would find out.

She'd find out on Thursday at the Spring assembly.

And so would the rest of the school.

Beast tried to think.

What could they do?

"Hey," Matthew said. "Look who's going into the A&P."

"Holly," said Beast. "And Joanne."

He ducked into the doorway of Wuff Wuff's Pet Store.

Holly didn't have to know he had crossed Linden Avenue.

She was the world's worst tattletale.

Besides, she had screamed all over the place about that rabbit.

He swallowed.

He had just remembered his birthday party.

Holly wasn't so bad after all.

Matthew gave him a poke. "Is that a pair of Mr. Hunt's pants?" He pointed. "Back there on the sidewalk?"

Beast turned.

He put the rest of the clothes down in front of Wuff Wuff's.

He raced along the street. He scooped up the pants.

A moment later they turned in at Handy Andy's Cleaners.

They threw Mr. Hunt's clothes up on the counter.

"Hey," said Beast. "I just thought of something." He started to sing. "No more goo with Stick On Glue."

He sang under his breath though.

He was a terrible singer.

Matthew looked at him. "What?"

Mrs. Andy was looking at him too. "When do you need these things?"

Matthew raised one shoulder in the air. "I don't know. Next month?"

"I'm not going to keep this stuff forever," Mrs. Andy said. "Thursday or Friday?"

"Sure," said Matthew. "Make it Thursday."

He turned to Beast. "We might be able to get more money for picking everything up. The sooner the better."

Matthew took the cleaning ticket and put it in his pocket. Then they walked out of the store.

"This is what I think," Beast said. He

rubbed his hands on his jeans. "We can get some of that glue."

Matthew started to sing the song. "No more gooooo . . ."

"Hey, guys," yelled someone. "Wait up."

It was Timothy Barbiero. "Where are you going?"

Beast looked toward the A&P. "We have to get glue for something."

Timothy nodded. "I have to get halibut."

"What's—" Beast began.

Timothy pinched his nose with his fingers. 'Fish."

They started down the street.

Matthew was making gagging noises. He made believe he was falling as they opened he door to the A&P.

"I can't wait for Easter vacation," Timothy said. "No school. And I'm going to my grandmother's."

"I hope you're not going to miss my party," said Beast.

Matthew nodded. "Beast has the best sister in the world."

"Holly?" Timothy asked, surprised.

"You haven't heard about the surprise party?" Matthew asked. "Everyone's invited."

"Don't worry," said Timothy. "I'll be there. Even if I have to come home from my grandmother's."

Beast started toward the stationery section. He felt a little worried.

Suppose Holly was going to have only a couple of kids?

Everyone's feelings would be hurt.

No one would talk to him for the rest of the year.

Just then he spotted her.

She and Joanne were in the soda section.

He ducked behind a stack of cans to watch them.

It was a good thing he had done all that Leko practicing.

He moved as fast as lightning.

Then he took a deep breath.

Holly and Joanne were loading piles of sod
cans into a cart.

She must be having tons of kids.

It looked like enough soda for his whol
class.

Chapter 6

The "no more goo" glue hadn't worked.

It hadn't worked at all.

Beast and Matthew had sneaked into the auditorium at lunchtime.

The monster rabbit was standing there on the stage. It looked as if his head were bent over backward.

Now there was glue on his cotton-ball fur.

There was glue on his carrot.

And there was glue all over Beast's new spring jacket.

He wasn't worried about the jacket though.

He was worried about Mrs. Kettle.

What would happen when she got a look at the Easter Rabbit?

Right now it was raining out. Pouring.

Too bad he didn't have a yellow raincoat like Matthew's.

His was stuck up in his closet somewhere. It was so small he couldn't even move in it.

He wouldn't wear it if you paid him a million dollars.

He grabbed a fat stick.

He tossed it into the water that raced along next to the curb.

He raced after it.

So did Matthew.

The stick bobbed in the water. Then it stopped. It was caught in a tangle of leaves.

Beast gave it a kick with one foot.

The water seeped into his sneakers.

"Yeow!" he yelled. "Freezing."

In back of them, a voice yelled.

Holly was leaning out the window. "Richard," she shouted. "You'd better come in here. Where's your raincoat? Mother's going to kill you."

Beast didn't answer.

He watched the stick sail down the drain.

"It's going out to sea," Matthew said.

"Probably to China," said Beast. "Or maybe Florida."

Holly stuck her head out a little farther. "I'm supposed to be baby-sitting you, Richard. Do you want me to get in trouble?"

He stuck out his front teeth and made claws with his hands.

Matthew gave him a poke. "Hap-py birthday to youuuuuuuu," he sang under his breath.

Beast spread out his fingers.

He waved at Holly.

"Coming right now."

He looked at Matthew. "Let's get something to eat."

Inside, the kitchen was a mess.

Holly and Joanne were making no-cook cookies.

They were the worst cookies in the world.

All they were was a pile of cereal and marshmallows that stuck to your teeth.

". . . feel terrible," Holly was saying. "My egg—I mean my jewelry carton—all smashed."

Beast looked out the window.

"I must have stepped on it." Holly looked at him. "Don't take a cookie. Don't even think of it."

"Don't worry, I won't." Beast couldn't believe it. Holly didn't know he had ruined her carton.

What luck!

The one he had made for her was still in the classroom. He'd throw it out right after Easter.

"We have to save these cookies," Joanne said.

"Hap-py birth-day," Matthew hummed.

Beast smiled. Too bad they were such horrible cookies.

He opened the refrigerator door.

"Beast likes chocolate chips the best." Matthew grinned at Beast. "I'll take a soda."

"Rots the teeth out of your head," Joanne said.

"Chocolate chips do that?" Beast asked.

"No, soda," said Joanne.

Matthew popped off the soda top. He began to drink.

"Don't these kids ever drink out of a glass?" Joanne asked.

"Worst manners in the world." Holly reached into the cereal box. She stuck a handful of flakes in her mouth.

Beast looked at her. He knew what she was doing.

She was trying to make sure he didn't see the list on the table.

It said:

ice cream
soda

chips
pretzels
dip

Everything he loved.

He was really starting to like Holly. He took a quick sip of milk from the carton.

Holly stared at him. "Did you drink right out of the container? I can't stand—"

"I like chocolate chips too," said Matthew. "Why don't you put them on the list?"

Beast made believe he hadn't heard Matthew.

What was that matter with that kid, anyway?

Beast pulled out a package of bread.

Matthew was leaning over the table.

He was whispering something to Holly.

Beast worked his hand down inside the package. He tried to get a fat middle slice.

"Invite Noah Green?" he heard Holly say. "What are you talking about?"

know him?" Joanne asked. "Is he

"Noah Green?" Holly started to laugh. He's one of the idiots in Beast's class."

Joanne started to laugh too.

She opened her mouth wide.

Beast could see she had cereal and marshmallow stuck to her braces.

"Noah Green is the smartest kid in the class," Matthew said. "I wouldn't leave him out if I were you."

Holly stopped laughing. "What—"

"You can't have a surprise party for Beast and leave out Noah," Matthew said.

Holly started to laugh again.

She and Joanne looked like a pair of hyenas, Beast thought.

"He thinks—" Holly was laughing so hard she could hardly get the words out. "He thinks—"

"They must be crazy," said Joanne.

"You're not having a party for Beast?" Matthew asked.

"I'm having a spring party," said Holly. "For some of the kids in my class. Not for—"

Beast didn't wait to hear any more.

He grabbed his jacket. He raced outside in the rain.

Chapter 7

This was the worst day of Beast's life.

He hadn't said one word to Holly since yesterday.

He hadn't even taken the two jelly beans she had left on his dresser.

He wished he could disappear like Leko the Lizard Man.

Right now he was supposed to be writing a story. A Happy Spring story.

There was a substitute teacher today.

A new one.

She said she loved story writing.

Beast hated to think about spring. It reminded him of that rabbit business.

He had peeked in the auditorium this morning.

The rabbit's head had tilted forward.

It was leaning over its chest.

The carrot seemed to be missing.

Noah Green tapped him on the shoulder.

Noah didn't look very happy either. "I didn't get an invitation to your party yet," he said.

Timothy leaned across the aisle. "I didn't either."

"The party's off," Beast said. "It was a mistake."

"What?" Timothy said. "I even told my grandmother."

"Some vacation this will be," said Noah.

"I hope we're all writing wonderful stories," the teacher said.

Beast stared at his paper.

He made believe he was thinking.

He wrote his first sentence.

A rabbit was hopping.

Then he stopped.
He couldn't think of another thing to say.
He stood up and took the pass.
He went down the hall.
Today was Thursday.
This afternoon was assembly.
Mrs. Kettle would take one look at tha
rabbit.
She'd start screaming.
He looked out the window.
A bunch of robins were hanging around or
the lawn. They were looking for worms.
What would happen if he ran away?
What would happen if he just opened the
door? He could walk down Polk Street. He
could disappear around the corner.
Beast pushed at the door.
It smelled good outside.
He didn't even need a jacket.
He looked down the hall.

Mrs. Gates was putting flowers on the bulletin board.

She was standing on a chair.

Beast took a breath. He pushed the door open farther.

Then he was outside. Running amuck, he told himself, really running amuck.

He raced past the flagpole.

In back of him were all the school windows.

He hoped the principal, Mr. Mancina, wasn't looking out.

He hoped the substitute teacher wasn't either.

What would they do if they saw him?

Up ahead was the corner.

He pounded down the street toward it.

He could hardly breathe.

In front of him was a garbage can cover.

He jumped over it.

The next thing he knew he was on the ground.

There was a hole in the knee of his jeans.

His knee was bleeding.

He stood up and kept going.

A moment later, he was around the corner.

He couldn't see the school anymore.

He was safe.

Almost safe.

The postman was halfway down the street.

Beast crossed over to the other side.

His knee was stinging.

His nose was running too.

He felt like sitting on the curb and crying like a baby.

He looked down the street.

He didn't even know where he could go.

Chapter 8

Beast turned in at the park.

It was almost empty.

Benny, the park man, was down at the other end, sweeping.

A woman was throwing bread to a bunch of birds.

Beast had a pain in his side from running. He stopped to catch his breath.

Then he heard footsteps.

Someone was coming fast.

He started to run again.

He headed for the trees.

Someone must be after him.

Maybe Mr. Mancina had called the police.

He wondered what they did with kids who ran away.

He had never heard of someone taking off just before lunch.

Not even Drake Evans, the worst boy in the Polk Street School.

"Wait a minute," someone yelled.

Holly?

Was that Holly?

He looked back over his shoulder.

It *was* Holly.

She was breathing hard, as hard as he was.

She was holding her side too.

"Richard?" Holly called. "Will you just—"

He stopped running.

Holly was close now.

Her face was red. Her hair was flying around.

For a moment he stared at her.

Her face looked good to him.

He was glad to see her.

He didn't say anything though.

He knew he was going to cry.

If Holly saw him crying, he'd—

He turned and walked away from her.

"Richard," Holly said. "You're going to be in terrible trouble."

He shook his head. "I don't care," he said. "I'm never going back to school again."

He blinked hard. "Hey." He turned around. "Why are *you* running away?"

Holly sank down, she leaned against a tree.

"Why do you think?" she asked. "I was sitting there doing social studies. Then I looked out the window."

Beast sat down too. He picked up a stone. He rolled it around in his hands.

"I saw you," Holly said. "I got so afraid. Suppose someone else saw you? Suppose Mr. Mancina saw you—?" She broke off. "Your hands are filthy from that stone."

Beast tossed the stone at a tree.

He looked at his hands.

Holly was right.

They were full of mud.

He wiped them on his shirt, thinking.

Holly said she was afraid.

He couldn't believe it. Holly was worried about him.

It made him feel great. He wanted to smile. He wanted to laugh.

He looked up at the tree branches over his head. They were still bare. But soon they would have tiny green leaves.

Everything smelled good.

"Why are you smiling, Richard?" Holly asked. "Are you crazy?"

Beast shook his head.

Then Holly leaned forward. He could see about a hundred freckles on her cheeks.

"Listen, Richard," she said. "That party was for all girls. Girls. Not one boy. You would hate an all-girl party."

"I didn't know that," he said.

She leaned forward. "I'm going to tell you

something else, Richard," she said. "You're the worst pain in the world. You're a mess. Look at you. You've got mud all over."

Beast took a another swipe at his shirt.

Holly even had freckles on her forehead, Beast thought. She probably had a thousand altogether.

"But you know what, Richard?" Holly said. She looked as if she were ready to cry. "You're a good kid." She stopped for a moment. "And I'm glad you're my brother."

Beast took a breath of good spring air.

All of Holly's freckles didn't look bad, he thought. They didn't look bad at all.

If only the rabbit's head hadn't fallen off.

If only they weren't going to be in such trouble for running away.

Otherwise it would have been a great day.

Chapter 9

For a few minutes they sat there. Then Holly sighed. "Why are you running away anyway?" she asked.

"The rabbit," Beast said. "Mrs. Kettle's Easter Rabbit."

Holly's mouth looked like a round O. "I forgot all about that."

Beast raised his head. "What's that noise?"

"Kids," Holly said. "Kids yelling."

Beast thought about it a moment. Everyone had eaten lunch by now. They were out in the schoolyard.

He wondered who knew he was gone.

Matthew.

Timothy Barbiero.

Maybe the substitute teacher.

He hoped she hadn't called the police.

He could feel his stomach rumble. "I'm hungry," he said.

Holly clicked her teeth. "How could you be hungry? We're in all this trouble."

Beast raised one shoulder in the air.

"We have to go back." Holly stood up. "Right now."

Beast looked up at her. "I'm never going back."

Holly smiled a little. "You'll starve to death out here."

"I don't care."

He could feel his stomach rumble again.

He knew he had to go back anyway.

He couldn't stay in the park forever.

Holly leaned over. "Come on, Richard. You have to tell Mrs. Kettle. I'll even go with you."

"You'll go with me?" he asked. He picked up another stone.

He threw it against a tree.

He was never going to get mad at Holly again.

He stood up too.

"What can I say to her?" he asked.

"We'll think of it when we get there," Holly said.

Beast followed her out of the park.

They crossed the street and went down the block.

In the schoolyard, the boys were playing ball.

Beast didn't stop though. He and Holly went straight into school.

They walked up the stairs to Mrs. Kettle's room.

Mrs. Kettle was writing on the blackboard.

Half a peanut butter sandwich was on her desk.

Beast could see she was still chewing.

Holly cleared her throat. "My brother wants to tell you something," she said.

Mrs. Kettle wiped the chalk off her fingers. She looked at Beast.

She was frowning a little.

He tried to open his mouth.

His tongue seemed to be stuck.

"Well?" Mrs. Kettle asked.

Holly gave him a poke.

"The rabbit," he said.

Mrs. Kettle frowned a little more. "What rabbit?"

Beast didn't say anything.

Holly cleared her throat again. "The rabbit, the one on the stage."

Mrs. Kettle nodded. "Yes."

"His head—" Beast said. He thought his voice sounded odd. Dry.

He raised his hands as if he had a ball. "The head—"

Mrs. Kettle reached for her sandwich.

"Aren't you the boy who's always yelling outside?"

"Yes," said Holly. "That's Richard."

"Speak up," said Mrs. Kettle.

Beast took a breath. "Somehow. We were— Anyway, the head fell off."

Everything was quiet.

Beast could hear the kids in the schoolyard.

Then he heard another sound.

He looked at Mrs. Kettle.

It was the first time he had ever seen her laugh.

"Richard," she said. "That rabbit has been losing his head for as long as I've been here. And that's a long time."

Probably a hundred years, Beast thought.

Next to him, he heard Holly say, "All this trouble for nothing."

"Trouble?" Mrs. Kettle asked.

"Worrying," said Holly. "Running away."

Mrs. Kettle closed her eyes for a moment.

"Good thing you came back. It would be terrible to miss the Spring assembly."

Beast nodded.

He and Holly started out the door.

"Wait," said Mrs. Kettle. "Let me give you notes for your teachers. Explain this whole mess."

Mrs. Kettle frowned at them. "Don't ever run away again. You always have to come back."

She picked up her sandwich again.

Beast followed Holly outside.

He was starving.

He was going right back to the classroom and get his lunch.

He took a good look at Holly.

There was something else he was going to do.

He was going to get the egg carton he had made.

Everyone said it was the best in his class.

It would be great for Holly's jewelry.

He started for the classroom.

Wait till he told Matthew that Mrs. Kettle had laughed.

Matthew would never believe it.